for Alison and Caroline

First published in Great Britain in 1985 by A & C Black.
This paperback edition published in 2000 by Andersen Press Ltd.,
20 Vauxhall Bridge Road, London SW1V 2SA.
Published in Australia by Random House Australia Pty.,
20 Alfred Street, Milsons Point, Sydney, NSW 2061.
All rights reserved.

Printed and bound in Italy by Grafiche AZ, Verona.

10   9   8   7   6   5   4

British Library Cataloguing in Publication Data available.

ISBN 0 86264 756 8
ISBN 978 0 86264 756 8

This book has been printed on acid-free paper

What's Inside?

THE ALPHABET BOOK
by
Satoshi Kitamura

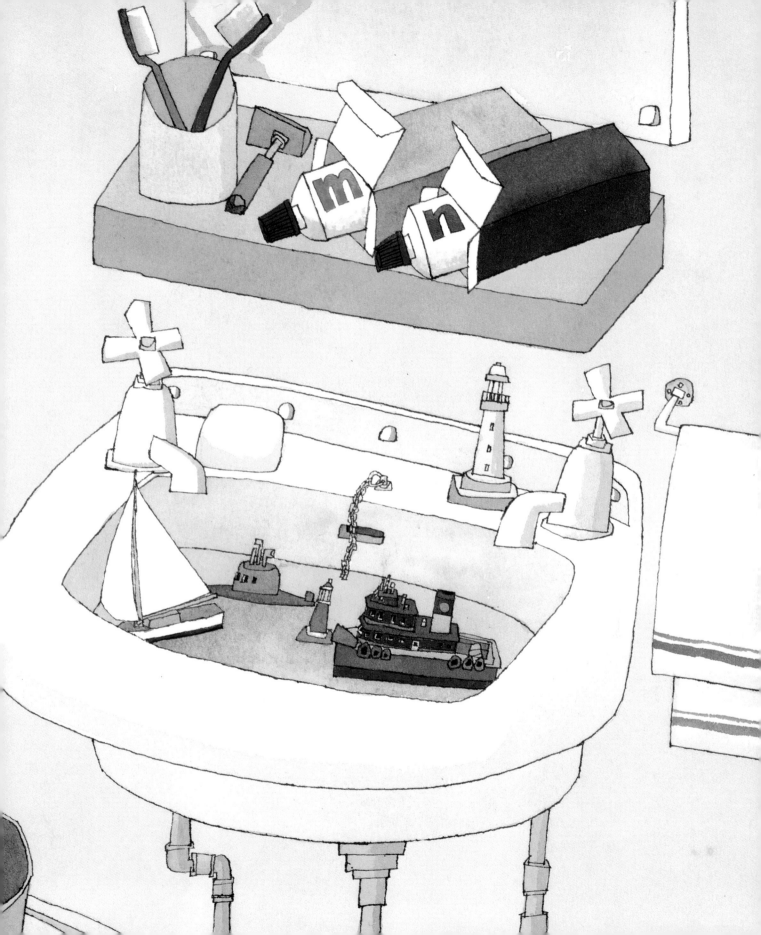

Snow
and
tiger

Woodpecker
and
Xylophone

Yacht and **Zebra**

Some other titles illustrated by Satoshi Kitamura

Sheep in Wolves' Clothing
Goldfish Hide-and-Seek
Me and My Cat?
In the Attic by Hiawyn Oram
Angry Arthur by Hiawyn Oram

Board books:
Cat is Sleepy, Duck is Dirty, Dog is Thirsty and *Squirrel is Hungry*
Bathtime Boots and *A Friend for Boots*